Disney's
Mulan

Ladybird

Early one morning, long long ago, a young Chinese girl sat on her bedroom floor, reading aloud from a scroll. She took up her brush and began to write the words on her arm: *quiet and demure… graceful… polite…*

She stopped to eat some breakfast and then continued with her mouth full: *refined… poised…*

This was Mulan! She was seventeen years old and daughter of Fa Zhou, a famous Chinese soldier. Mulan loved her family and always wanted to please them. But her high spirits often got her into trouble.

Today was very important. She was going to meet the Matchmaker with the other girls in the village. A good match in marriage would bring honour to her family, and she wanted to be well prepared. She dipped her brush into the ink and added one last thing: *punctual…*

But then she heard the cock crow. She was late already and there was a lot to do before she could leave.

Fa Zhou was busy praying in the Family Temple, "Honourable Ancestors, please help Mulan to impress the Matchmaker today." He heard a noise and stepped outside, where Mulan nearly knocked him over.

"Father, I've brought your tea," she explained.

"But you should already be in town," Fa Zhou told her. "We're counting on you..."

"...to uphold the family honour," Mulan interrupted, with a big grin. "Don't worry. I won't let you down. Wish me luck."

Then she hurried off to get her father's horse, Khan.

Fa Zhou watched them ride away. "I'm going to pray some more," he decided, and went back into the Temple.

Over in the village, rickshaws and carts bustled down the road. And Fa Li, Mulan's mother, waited anxiously for her daughter. She spotted Grandmother Fa carrying a cricket cage across the road.

All around her, carts and horses swerved and collided. But, miraculously, Grandmother Fa reached the other side safely and announced, “Yes, this cricket is a lucky one!”

Suddenly they heard some familiar hooves. “I’m here!” shouted Mulan, as she brought Khan to a halt.

Fa Li looked crossly at her untidy daughter. But there was no time to talk. She pushed the girl straight into the freezing bathtub… then on to the hairdressers’… the dressmakers’… and the make-up shop. Soon Mulan was transformed and she joined the line of girls outside the Matchmaker’s house.

At noon the Matchmaker called out sternly, “Fa Mulan!” Once inside, the Matchmaker silently circled the girl and made notes. “Now pour the tea,” she ordered. At that moment, the little cricket, Cri-Kee, escaped and hopped into the teacup. Mulan tried to grab him, but spilt the tea.

The Matchmaker’s dress caught fire. She jumped back and ran out screaming, “You may look like a bride, but you will never bring honour to your family!”

As Mulan made her way home, she thought about what the Matchmaker had said. Mulan looked sadly at her reflection in the Temple. She knew that the painted girl looking back at her was not her true self. But she didn't want to disgrace her family.

Mulan went sadly into the garden, where Fa Zhou came to find her. "My, what beautiful blossoms we have this year," he said, softly. "When this one blooms, it will be the most beautiful of all."

Mulan smiled. She knew he had forgiven her.

Suddenly drums sounded, there was bad news. The Huns had invaded China. By order of the Emperor, one man from every family was called to serve in the Imperial Army. Fa Zhou had to prepare to leave the next day.

But Mulan hated the thought that her aging father would be harmed. So that night she stole her father's army papers, cut off her hair and got dressed in his armour. Then she saddled Khan and rode out into the darkness.

She had taken Fa Zhou's place in the Emperor's Army.

As wind gusted through the Fa Family Temple, the voice of the First Ancestor echoed in the shadows, "Mushu… awake!"

A tiny dragon emerged and banged a gong. Straightaway the room filled with quarrelling ghosts, each blaming another for Mulan's actions. But they were all agreed on one thing – Mulan would need the most powerful Guardian of all to protect her.

Mushu proudly stood forward, certain they meant him. But the Ancestors just laughed. They wouldn't choose Mushu again. He'd made a big mistake last time. No, Mushu's job was to go and wake the Great Stone Dragon.

Reluctantly Mushu marched outside to the enormous old statue and banged his gong again. There was no response. So Mushu climbed up and banged the statue on the head. CRRUUNCH! The whole thing crumbled to the ground.

So, fearing the Ancestors' anger, Mushu held the huge stone head over his own and pretended to be the Great Stone Dragon.

"Go!" commanded the First Ancestor. "The fate of the Fa Family rests in your claws."

Mushu and Cri-Kee found Mulan on a cliff overlooking the Imperial Army Training Camp. “Who am I fooling?” she sighed. “It’s going to take a miracle to get me into the Army.”

“Did I hear someone ask for a miracle!” asked Mushu. “Your serpentine salvation is at hand!” Then he explained that he was the Guardian, sent by her Ancestors.

Mulan wasn’t convinced. However, since she needed all the help she could get, Mulan followed the little dragon’s advice and went to sign in at the Army Camp.

Mushu hid in her collar, telling her what to say to the other soldiers. But Mushu got it wrong and soon the whole Camp was in chaos. Then they came face to face with angry Captain Shang.

“Show me your army papers!” he ordered Mulan. He was shocked to discover that the Great Fa Zhou had a son. But he accepted it and told the recruits to tidy up.

Mulan’s secret was safe, for the moment…

The next day the training began. Captain Shang shot an arrow to the top of a high pole. Then he ordered each of the recruits in turn to climb up to get it. But none of them could. The heavy weights tied to their wrists made it almost impossible.

"We've got a long way to go," grumbled the Captain, and he tossed them some wooden poles to use as weapons.

Some of the soldiers tried to make fun of Mulan. One put an insect down her neck and she dropped her pole.

"You haven't got a clue, have you!" shouted the Captain, and Mulan got the blame again.

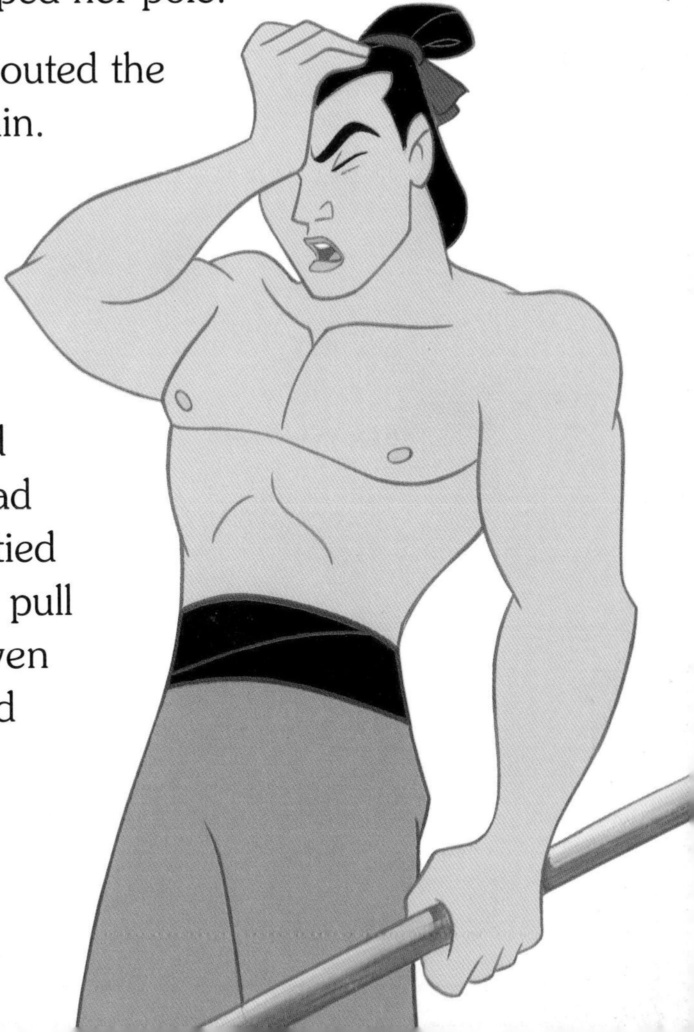

The tough training continued and, before long, Mulan was exhausted. She collapsed, and Captain Shang told her to go home.

Mulan turned to leave. But she spotted the arrow at the top of the pole and had an idea. Determined to try again, she tied the weights together and used them to pull herself up. Everyone admired her, even Captain Shang, and she was welcomed back into the Camp.

Once the training was complete, it was time to join the Main Army in the mountains. But the enemy had arrived before them. Signs of a fierce battle lay all around – the Emperor's Army had been destroyed. Then, as Shang ordered his soldiers to move out, they too were attacked by the enemy. Thousands of Hun warriors charged over the hilltop – led by their commander, the powerful Shan-Yu!

"Prepare to fight!" ordered Shang. "If we die, we die with honour. Aim the cannon at Shan-Yu!"

But Mulan had another idea. She ran forward and fired the cannon into a snowy mountain ridge, triggering off an avalanche.

Snow crashed down onto the Huns, but Shan-Yu still charged ahead. Wanting revenge, he struck Mulan with his sword, but was then engulfed in the snow.

Khan raced to rescue Mulan and together they helped to save Captain Shang. The Imperial Army was safe, and Mulan was proclaimed the battle hero. But soon she collapsed in pain.

Mulan awoke in the doctor's tent. Surrounded by angry faces, she knew at once that her secret had been discovered. Fa Zhou's *son* was in fact a girl, and it was the Captain's duty to execute her.

But Shang refused. Throwing the sword down, he said, "A life for a life. My debt is repaid." Then he ordered his troops to move out.

Mulan was left in the mountains with Mushu, Cri-Kee and Khan.

"I should never have left home," Mulan murmured. "I'm sorry I wasted your time, Mushu."

"You didn't!" said the little dragon, embarrassed. "The truth is, we're both frauds. Your Ancestors never sent me. They don't even like me. But we're in this together and that's how we'll finish it."

Suddenly a terrifying howl echoed round the mountains, and they watched in horror as Shan-Yu and five Hun warriors climbed out of the snow. Then they followed them to the Imperial City.

Mulan caught up with Shang just as he and his troops were approaching the Imperial Palace. She tried to warn him that the Emperor was in danger. But Shang still felt betrayed by Mulan and he refused to trust her again.

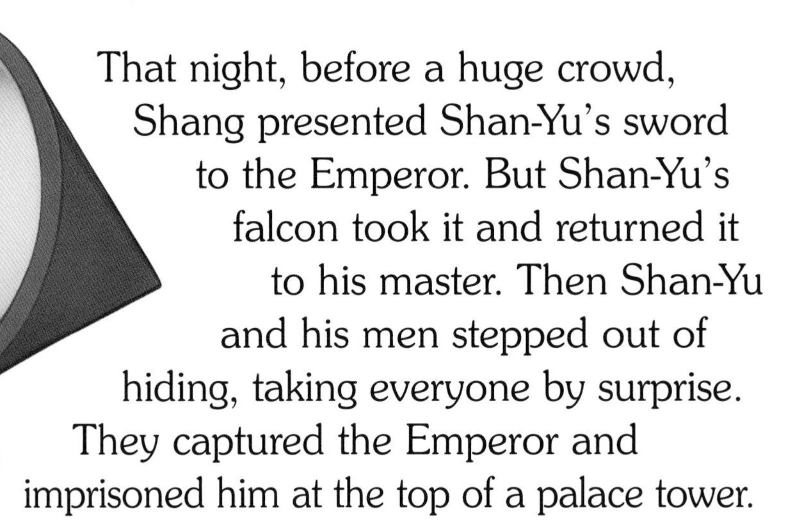

That night, before a huge crowd, Shang presented Shan-Yu's sword to the Emperor. But Shan-Yu's falcon took it and returned it to his master. Then Shan-Yu and his men stepped out of hiding, taking everyone by surprise. They captured the Emperor and imprisoned him at the top of a palace tower.

Thinking quickly, Mulan decided what to do. She asked three of the Captain's soldiers, Yao, Ling and Chien-Po, to help her. Disguised as palace maidens, they made their way up the tower. And Shang agreed to help them.

The 'girls' knocked out the Hun guards and whisked the Emperor away to safety, whilst Shang faced Shan-Yu. Furious that the Emperor had escaped, Shan-Yu put his sword to Shang's neck.

But Mulan called to Shan-Yu. He recognised her at once and let Shang go. Shan-Yu chased Mulan out onto the rooftop, where he trapped her near the edge.

"It looks like you're out of ideas," he sneered.

"Not quite!" answered Mulan. "Ready, Mushu?"

"I'm ready!" cried the little dragon. Then Cri-Kee lit the rocket that was strapped to Mushu's back.

It took off towards Shan-Yu, sending him crashing into the munitions tower.

Mulan grabbed Mushu and Cri-Kee and then ran with all her might to get off the roof.

Fireworks exploded in all directions and a giant fireball engulfed the palace. The force of the blast sent Captain Shang flying down some steps, and seconds later Mulan landed on top of him. She hugged him, glad to see he was safe. Mushu and Cri-Kee dropped down beside them.

Suddenly the Emperor approached. He spoke sternly to Mulan, "I've heard a great deal about you, Fa Mulan," he said. "You stole your father's armour, ran away from home, impersonated a soldier, deceived your commanding officer, dishonoured the Imperial Army, destroyed my palace and..."

Mulan looked down, shaking with fear.

"You have saved us all!" the Emperor went on, and smiled.

Then he did something amazing. The Emperor and everyone else bowed to Mulan... and he presented Mulan with his medallion and Shan-Yu's sword to honour her family.

The next day Mulan presented the Emperor's gifts to her father. But he just put them aside and hugged her. "The greatest gift is having you for a daughter."

At that moment Shang came into the garden and, to the delight of the entire family, Mulan invited him to dinner.

Meanwhile, in the Temple, Mushu was made a Family Guardian. "Call out for eggrolls!" he cried. It was time to celebrate.